Dear Parent:

Congratulations! Your child is taking the first steps on an exciting journey. The destination? Independent reading!

STEP INTO READING® will help your child get there. The program offers five steps to reading success. Each step includes fun stories and colorful art. There are also Step into Reading Sticker Books, Step into Reading Math Readers, Step into Reading Write-In Readers, Step into Reading Phonics Readers, and Step into Reading Phonics First Steps! Boxed Sets—a complete literacy program with something for every child.

Learning to Read, Step by Step!

Ready to Read Preschool–Kindergarten
• big type and easy words • rhyme and rhythm • picture clues
For children who know the alphabet and are eager to begin reading.

Reading with Help Preschool–Grade 1
• basic vocabulary • short sentences • simple stories
For children who recognize familiar words and sound out new words with help.

Reading on Your Own Grades 1–3
• engaging characters • easy-to-follow plots • popular topics
For children who are ready to read on their own.

Reading Paragraphs Grades 2–3
• challenging vocabulary • short paragraphs • exciting stories
For newly independent readers who read simple sentences with confidence.

Ready for Chapters Grades 2–4
• chapters • longer paragraphs • full-color art
For children who want to take the plunge into chapter books but still like colorful pictures.

STEP INTO READING® is designed to give every child a successful reading experience. The grade levels are only guides. Children can progress through the steps at their own speed, developing confidence in their reading, no matter what their grade.

Remember, a lifetime love of reading starts with a single step!

For flower girls Louise, Annie,
Eliza, Jordan, and Chloe
—M.M.

To my little niece Auréliane
—C.G.

Copyright © 2007 by Megan McDonald
Illustrations copyright © 2007 by Claudine Gevry

All rights reserved. Published in the United States by Random House Children's Books, a division of Random House, Inc., New York.

STEP INTO READING, RANDOM HOUSE, and the Random House colophon are registered trademarks of Random House, Inc.

www.stepintoreading.com

Educators and librarians, for a variety of teaching tools, visit us at www.randomhouse.com/teachers

Library of Congress Cataloging-in-Publication Data
McDonald, Megan.
Daisy Jane, best-ever flower girl / by Ann Megan McDonald ;
illustrated by Claudine Gevry. — 1st ed.
    p. cm. — (Step into reading. Step 3 book)
ISBN 978-0-375-83110-2 (trade pbk.) — ISBN 978-0-375-93110-9 (lib. bdg.)
SUMMARY: Daisy Jane, who is thrilled to be the flower girl at her babysitter's wedding, helps save the day when a storm threatens the festivities.
[1. Weddings—Fiction. 2. Flower girls—Fiction.] I. Gevry, Claudine, ill. II. Title. III. Title: Daisy Jane best ever flower girl. IV. Series.
PZ7.M478419Dai 2007 [E]—dc22 2006009104

Printed in the United States of America

10 9 8 7 6 5 4 3 2 1

First Edition

Daisy Jane

Best-Ever Flower Girl!

by Megan McDonald
illustrated by Claudine Gevry

Random House 🏠 New York

Chapter One

Allie was Daisy's best babysitter.
They liked to play Superheroes.
They liked to play Princesses.

Most of all,

they liked to play Brides.

Sometimes Daisy was the bride.

Sometimes Daisy was

the flower girl.

Mr. Moon was always the groom.

Daisy had a swirly bride dress.

Daisy had a twirly wedding ring.

Daisy had a basket

filled with paper flowers.

Daisy wore an old curtain
for her veil.
She had
a new lucky-charm bracelet.

She borrowed

Allie's pink shoes.

And she had

a blue velvet ribbon for her hair.

She even had a fake cake

with roses and people on top.

But there was one thing

Daisy did not have.

Daisy did not have . . .

a real wedding!

Chapter Two

"Hi, Daisy Jane!" said Allie.

"Hi, Alley Cat!" said Daisy.

"I have a surprise for you,"
  said Allie.

"Is it a kitten?" asked Daisy.

"Better," said Allie.

Daisy could not think of *anything*
better than a kitten.

"I'm getting married!" said Allie.

"We can play Brides *for real*—

if you will be my flower girl.

What do you say?"

Flower girl! A real wedding!

Weddings were even better

than kittens!

"I say YES!" said Daisy.

"I say YAHOO!"

She jumped up and down.

She twirled round and round.

She hugged Allie tight.

"I hope you have someone to marry besides a cat," she said.

"His name is Rick," said Allie.

"Do you promise to love him?" asked Daisy.

"I do," said Allie.

"Even when he's old and wrinkled? And when he has chicken pox?"

"I do," said Allie.

"Will there be a long white dress
and gold rings
and lots and lots of flowers?"
"Yes," said Allie.

"Will there be finger sandwiches
and a fancy cake
with roses and people on top?
And lots and lots of presents?"

"Yes," said Allie.

"There will be a garden

and a big tent.

We'll dance under the stars.

And . . . there will be fireworks!"

17

"But most of all, there will be you.

Daisy Jane,

the best-ever flower girl!"

Chapter Three

Allie took Daisy to find a dress.

A special flower-girl dress.

There were dresses
with puffy sleeves
and ruffly knees.

There were dresses
with itchy lace
and too-tight waists.

There were dresses
with rows and rows
of bows.

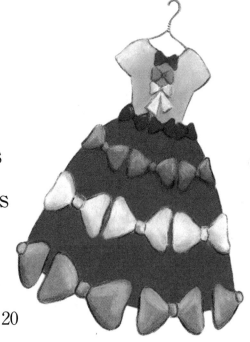

Then ... they saw it.

A blue-sky dress

with tiny pink flowers.

It was not too poofy, not too goofy.

Not too itchy, not too pinchy.

It did not have too many bows.

And it fit just right.

Daisy tried on her new dress.

She pranced and danced

around the house

in her new blue

best-ever flower-girl dress.

"Dum dum dee dum!"

Allie showed Daisy
how to march down the hall,
slow as ketchup.
Daisy tossed flowers
to the left and to the right.
"Perfect," said Allie.

Chapter Four

At last! The big day!

Daisy wore her blue-sky dress

and a daisy chain in her hair.

Daisy wore her

good-luck charm bracelet.

"Dum dum dee dum!" sang Daisy.

"Hey, flower girl," said Allie.

"You look pretty as a daisy!"

"You too!" said Daisy.

She hugged the bride

without squishing her dress.

Allie looked up at the clouds.

"Please don't rain!

I want this day to be perfect!"

The bride fixed her veil.

The bride picked up her flowers.

The bride took her dad's arm.

"Let's get married, everybody!"

said Allie.

Daisy walked down
the garden path,
slow as ketchup.
She tossed rose petals
to the left and to the right.
The bride floated down the aisle
on a bed of rose petals.

She promised to love the groom

even if he had chicken pox.

The wedding was beautiful.

Until . . . all of a sudden
puffy gray clouds moved
across the sun.
The sky turned dark.
The wind blew up.

It blew the hat off of
old Mrs. Winters.
It blew the flowers out of
their vases.
It blew dresses up
and tree branches down.

It blew umbrellas inside out.
Hats and flowers and ribbons
swirled and twirled
through the air.
BA-boom! Thunder!
Drip. Drip. Plip, plip, plip!

"RAIN!" shouted Daisy Jane.

"Big storm!"

"Run!"

"Everybody inside!"

The bride and groom

ran down the garden path.

SMASH!

Dishes went flying.

CRASH!

The big tent

blew over!

The big house was warm and cozy,
safe from the storm.
Everybody talked
and ate finger sandwiches.

They clinked spoons on glasses.

They said nice things

about the bride and groom.

Allie and Rick cut the fancy cake.

"Let's dance!" shouted the groom.

The music started.

Just then, *blink, wink, blink!*

The lights went out.

The music stopped.

The dancers stood like statues.

"My wedding!" cried Allie.

"No music!

No fireworks!

No dancing under the stars!"

Daisy Jane knew

just what to do.

Candles!

Everybody lit a candle.

Tiny flames glittered like stars.

Music!

Daisy played the piano.

Everybody danced

till they were warm and dry.

Fireworks!

Daisy passed out bubble wrap

from all the presents.

Pop! Pop! Pop-pop-pop-pop-pop!

It sounded just like fireworks.

For a little while, everybody forgot
about the storm.

"I'll never forget this day!"
said Allie.

"Not just because a big storm
came to my wedding!
Because you, Daisy Jane,
saved the day!"

When the storm passed
and the lights came back on,
Daisy got to dance
with the groom,
who was *not* a cat.

She stayed up as late as Cinderella.

At last, Daisy had a wedding.

A whirlwind of a wedding.

A perfect,

better-than-a-kitten wedding.

And she, Daisy Jane,
was the best-ever flower girl!